The Bug Box

The Backyard Adventures
of Charlotte and Madeline

Written by:
Dr. Debbie Salas-Lopez and Kristina Lopez Adduci

Illustrations by: Jamie Douglas

This book is dedicated to the 'apple of our eyes' – the twins that changed our lives - Charlotte and Madeline. We know no greater love than what we feel for you.

*In a big house in B'Town,
All covered with gnomes
Lived two twin girls
Who loved staying home.

When they woke in the morning,
The twins would smile and say,
"Grandma, Grandma,
Can we go out to play?"

Grandma dressed them
In their little blue pants
And out they would run
To bring in some ants.

The ants crawled and scurried

In and out of their socks

Giving poor Grandma

Quite a horrid shock.

Then one sunny day
Grandma declared
Let's get those girls
A bug box to share

Out ran the twins
The following day,
Collecting insects
To watch them play.

Into the box went
The beetles and slugs,
Fire flies and worms,
Bees and ladybugs.

"Oh my," cried the ant
what's this about?
"Why are we here?
As it tried to get out

18

"You don't look like me,"
The butterfly said
As she fluttered around
The ladybug's head.

19

20

"Don't get too huffy,"
Said the bees to the flies.
"We have this in common,
We can all see the sky."

"Hey, little girls,
Can you please set us free?
What will it take
For you to see?"

"We want to play freely
Like we did before,
But together this time
Friends forever more."

All the bugs gathered
To talk and be friends.
The ways they were different
Didn't matter in the end.

Charlotte and Madeline
Replied with a smile,
"We will release you
For a little while."

Out went the ants
And the rest close behind
Back into the yard
In two straight lines.

"Run, run," said the beetle.
"We have to hide.
We don't want them to catch us."
"No!" the butterfly cried.

The bugs stuck together
To watch the girls from afar.
Charlotte and Madeline
Cried, "Stay where you are!"

"We won't come to find you
You should stay free,
But please play together
And live in harmony."

Our similarities far outweigh our differences.